CAN YOU STOP A VOLCANIC DISASTER?

AN INTERACTIVE ECO ADVENTURE

BY MATT DOEDEN

CAPSTONE PRESS
a capstone imprint

You Choose Books are published by Capstone Press, an imprint of Capstone.
1710 Roe Crest Drive
North Mankato, Minnesota 56003
www.capstonepub.com

Library of Congress Cataloging-in-Publication Data
Names: Doeden, Matt, author.
Title: Can you stop a volcanic disaster? : an interactive eco adventure / Matt Doeden.
Description: North Mankato : Capstone Press, 2021. | Series: You choose:
   eco expeditions | Includes bibliographical references and index. | Audience: Ages
   8–11 | Audience: Grades 4–6
Identifiers: LCCN 2020039266 (print) | LCCN 2020039267 (ebook) |
   ISBN 9781496696007 (hardcover) | ISBN 9781496697080 (paperback) |
   ISBN 9781977153968 (eBook PDF)
Subjects: LCSH: Volcanoes—Juvenile literature. | Volcanic eruptions—Juvenile
   literature. | Seismology--Research--Juvenile literature.
Classification: LCC QE521.3 .D64 2021 (print) | LCC QE521.3 (ebook) |
   DDC 551.31—dc23
LC record available at https://lccn.loc.gov/2020039266
LC ebook record available at https://lccn.loc.gov/2020039267

Summary: The ground is shaking. A volcano is about the erupt. Hundreds of lives are
in danger. But you can help! Navigate through three different stories to discover what is
happening below Earth's surface. With dozens of story outcomes, it's up to you to stop a
volcanic disaster. The planet needs you. Will YOU CHOOSE to help?

Editorial Credits
Editors: Michelle Parkin and Aaron Sautter; Designer: Bobbie Nuytten;
Media Researcher: Kelly Garvin; Production Specialist: Katy LaVigne

Photo Credits
Newscom: Douglas Peebles/DanitaDelimont.com/"Danita Delimont Photography",
69, 77, Kris Tripplaar/Sipa USA, 6, Sergey Gorshkov/Minden Pictures, 31; Science
Source: Jeffrey Rotman, 86, NOAA/NSF/Woods Hole Oceanagraphic Institution, 93;
Shutterstock: Alexander Demyanenko, 62, Andrei Stepanov, 44, bierchen, cover (top),
backcover, 1 (t), Budkov Denis, 37, DeltaOFF, 48, Deni_Sugandi, 106 (bottom middle),
Ecuadorpostales, 107 (bottom), Egoreichenkov Evgenii, 106 (t), Ellen Bronstayn,
100 (b), fboudrias, 104-105, Matyas Rehak, 107 (top middle), Murloc, cover (b), 1
(b), 4, orxy, 107 (bm), Pedar Digre, 107 (t), Ralf Lehmann, 55, Sakarin Sawasdinaka,
106 (tm), SergeiEgorov, 106 (b), Sergey Krasnoshchokov, 17, Tomasz Wozniak, 12,
Travelphotopro, 78, tunasalmon, 106-107, VectorMine, 100 (t), Yongyut Kumsri, 21

Artistic elements: Shutterstock/Roman Bykhalov

All internet sites appearing in back matter were available and accurate when this book
was sent to press.

CHAPTER 1

PRESSURE BUILDING

"This way," says the young woman.

She leads you down a series of hallways at a brisk pace. You've just arrived by helicopter to the United States Geological Survey in Virginia. Everyone here looks deadly serious. The woman leads you into a conference room. People are seated around a long oval table. They stand as you enter the room.

"Hello, doctor," says a man in his late 50s. He introduces himself as Dr. Henderson, the director of the USGS.

You smile and nod. "I'm not a doctor yet," you remind him. You're actually a student, working on your doctorate in seismology.

Turn the page.

"Of course," he says. "But that doesn't matter right now. We understand that when it comes to the latest research, you're the expert."

You can't help but feel proud. Your research on earthquakes and creating models that predict volcanic activity has made waves in your field. You don't like to brag, but nobody else is better at discovering where and when a volcano might erupt.

A woman stands and gestures for you to take a seat at the table.

"Welcome. I'm Dr. Brooks, the head of research here at the USGS," she says. "We've been seeing an alarming level of seismic activity. It seems like a volcanic eruption, or series of eruptions, could be coming," she says.

"No need to catch me up," you say. Patience has never been your strength. "I know what's been happening. Earthquakes are occurring on the boundaries of the Pacific Plate. And there are small volcanic eruptions around the Ring of Fire, from Indonesia to Japan to South America."

Dr. Henderson interrupts. "It's more than just small eruptions. Some of the deep-sea eruptions have been much larger. The fact that they're so widespread is what concerns us. It's hard to tell where—and when—an eruption might take place. That makes it hard to warn anyone."

"Yes, I see," you reply, nodding. "With enough warning, we could get people out of harm's way."

"And that's why you're here," says Dr. Brooks. "If you can help us predict the eruptions, we can save many lives. The models that you helped create have changed the study of volcanic activity. They're far more accurate than anything we've had before. So we need you to tell us now: What is going to happen? Where will it happen, and when?"

You stand up, placing your palms on the table. "I can't tell you that. At least, not yet. I need more information. I need hard data."

"We'll provide whatever tools you need," Dr. Brooks says. "But we have to move quickly."

She's right about that. You've been following the news closely. The Earth is restless. The pressure is building. You glance at the map on the wall behind the table. It shows the locations of recent earthquakes. Some are near active volcanoes. Others are near dormant volcanoes, which haven't erupted in hundreds of years. You focus on several hot spots including Hawaii, Siberia, and the coast of Oregon.

"Our scientists tell us that we may not have long," Dr. Henderson says. "An airplane is ready to take you wherever you need to go. Today."

As you leave the room, you quickly send a text to Maria, who helped you develop your models. "Pack a bag," you type. "We have work to do."

To research a previously dormant volcano in Siberia, Russia, turn to page 13.

To investigate active volcanoes of Hawaii, turn to page 49.

To study an undersea volcano off the coast of Oregon, turn to page 79.

Mount Bolshaya Udina is part of a large group of volcanoes on Russia's Kamchatka Peninsula. The volcano was once thought extinct, but was reclassified as active in 2019.

CHAPTER 2

FIRE AND ICE

Brutally cold wind slaps you in the face as you hop out of the helicopter. Maria is right behind you. Before you stands a wind-swept, snow-covered mountain range. As the helicopter lifts away, it blasts stinging pellets of snow and ice at you.

"Come!" shouts a man dressed in a heavy parka. He pulls your arm.

You follow the man into the side of one of the mountains. Two large, metal doors open. They shut behind you with a CLANG.

It's warmer inside. You pull back your hood. The man who met you does the same. He has a long, slender face and thick black hair. You introduce yourselves.

Turn the page.

"Welcome to Siberia," he says with a thick accent. "I am Vladimir, but please call me Vlad. This is my research station." A young man and a young woman sit behind Vlad, typing on computers. "This is Nadya and Peter. They are graduate students from Moscow. They help me. I am sorry, but they do not speak English."

It's a small lab cut into the mountainside. Seismic equipment hums in the background. The heater that warms this place makes a low, constant buzz.

"I've been looking through some of your research on the flight," you tell Vlad as he shows you around. "Your work here is fascinating."

Vlad smiles. You can tell he's excited by the recent developments, and by the fact that you're here. He's clearly been at this outpost for quite a long time.

"Come," Vlad says. "Let me show you my latest data."

Vlad tells you what he's been observing. This chain of volcanoes has been dormant for a long time. But they appear to be waking up. As you look over Vlad's seismic data, you're amazed by what you see. Volcanoes once thought extinct are showing signs of life.

"You see," Vlad says.

You nod. "I do, Vlad. These readings . . . something is happening here. Magma is moving just a few miles below the surface. I wouldn't expect that here."

"Yes! Yes!" Vlad says. "We have not seen this before. Not until the last two weeks. I have sent reports to Moscow, but they do not understand how serious it is."

Turn the page.

Vlad leads you to a map of the area on a wall. Several dormant volcanoes lie along a fault line. Each of them glows in a bright color—blue, green, yellow. And one volcano pulses blood red.

"Tell me about that one," you say. Vlad smiles. "Yes. You do see it. Good, good." He explains that they've been measuring the pressure several miles below the surface. He says pressure is greatest below the volcano pulsing red. "Something is happening there," he says. "I think this volcano might be about to erupt."

Vlad has collected a lot of data. You could probably work from here. You can send the data to Isaac and the rest of your team back home. Isaac is your best data analyst. He might be able to build a better model of what's happening here. On the other hand, if you visit the volcano yourself, you might get even more detailed measurements.

The Kamchatka Peninsula in eastern Russia is one of the most geologically active areas in the world. It is home to 29 active volcanoes.

To study Vlad's data from the research station, turn to page 18.

To investigate the waking volcano yourself, turn to page 20.

You spend the next week pouring over the data from Vlad and his team. For the last month, temperatures under the surface have been on the rise. A series of small earthquakes has shaken the snow-covered land.

"We have never observed anything like this in Siberia," Vlad tells you.

Maria brings up the new model built by Isaac on her computer. She plugs in the new data and starts a simulation.

"Look at this," she tells Vlad. "It looks like part of the Pacific Plate is sinking, just a little bit. That's putting pressure on every fault nearby—even old, inactive faults like the one here."

Vlad peers at the model. "So this is not just happening in Siberia?"

You shake your head. "No. This could be affecting the entire region, from here to Japan. This isn't just one dormant volcano waking up."

As the two of you stare at the model, a sudden, deafening BOOM shakes the room. The ground trembles. Vlad's seismograph begins frantically tracing lines that show a powerful explosion nearby.

"What happened?" Vlad asks.

You think you already know. Normally, you would report what's happening to Dr. Brooks right away. But you are tempted to confirm your suspicions first.

To go outside to investigate, turn to page 23.
To call Dr. Brooks immediately, turn to page 24.

You tap the image of the waking volcano. "I think we should examine this up close, Vlad."

Vlad nods. "Yes. I thought that you might want to see it. Our transport is ready. Follow me."

Maria peers out from a work station. "I'm going to stay here," she says. "I want to go over these numbers more carefully and see what Isaac thinks."

Vlad leads you back outside into the blistering cold. Parked outside the research station are four small snowmobiles. Vlad gestures for you to take the one nearest the station. He climbs aboard another and starts the motor.

You do the same. You haven't ridden a snowmobile since you were twelve. But you remember how they work and start your motor. Vlad leads the way. With a twist of the throttle, you follow.

During winter, snowmobiles are the quickest way to cross Kamchatka's frozen landscape.

Gliding across the Siberian landscape is thrilling. It's a twisting and turning path through some of the most beautiful mountain scenery you've ever seen. In the distance you see a tall peak—the volcano. After a ride that lasts nearly an hour, you reach your destination.

Turn the page.

You climb off your snowmobiles and look up. The peak towers over you. The wind howls. You can't even hear each other speak. But Vlad gestures for you to follow. He leads you toward the rocky base of the mountain and into a hidden ice cave entrance. Once inside, the howling wind dies away.

"What is this place?" you ask.

Vlad points deeper into the cave. "Do you want to see what is happening? It is this way. But we must be careful."

As if to make Vlad's point, the ground begins to tremble beneath your feet. It's a small tremor, but it gets your attention. Is going into a cave at the base of a waking volcano really a good idea?

To go back to the research station, turn to page 26.
To continue into the volcano, turn to page 28.

You rush outside without even putting on your parka. As the door opens, a cold gust of air slams into your face. But you barely notice it. That's because you're looking at one of the most stunning and terrifying sights you've ever seen.

Several miles away, one of the previously dormant volcanoes has erupted. A cloud of smoke and ash fills the sky. Bright red lava rolls down the slope. As it hits snow and ice, it creates a wave of super-heated steam that rolls down the mountain.

And it's coming your way.

"Vlad! Maria!" you shout. "We have to go!"

All of your equipment and Vlad's critical data are inside. You can't bear the thought of leaving it all behind. But there's no telling how long you have—or if more eruptions will follow.

To run inside to collect your equipment, turn to page 30.
To grab your coat and run, turn to page 43.

"It's an eruption," you gasp.

It's the only explanation. In the corner, the needle on Vlad's seismograph is going crazy.

"Come quickly!" Vlad shouts from outside the research station. He's staring off in the distance with a terrified look on his face. "Lava is coming this way!"

You don't have time to go look just yet. You grab your phone and quickly dial Dr. Brooks. She picks up on the first ring.

"Dr. Brooks," you gasp. "One of the Siberian volcanoes just erupted. This isn't an isolated event. You need to put the entire region on alert."

"Yes, I agree!" Dr. Brooks responds. "We're seeing strong activity on our seismographs here, stretching all the way to Japan. I'll raise the alarm immediately."

Vlad is screaming. As you shove your phone into your pocket, you see why. A wall of lava and steam is rolling across the barren landscape— and it's headed your way.

"We have to go!" Vlad cries.

There's no time to grab Vlad's valuable research. All you can do is rush outside. Maria, Nadya, and Peter are close behind. Already, the cloud of super-heated steam is starting to blanket the area. Four snowmobiles are parked outside of the research station. Vlad is already on board one, with the motor running. Should you jump on with him? He's probably a more experienced driver than you. But the extra weight could slow you down.

To climb onto one of the other snowmobiles, turn to page 38.

To get onto the back of Vlad's snowmobile, turn to page 46.

You brace yourself, waiting for another tremor. But no more follow.

"That was a little one," Vlad says.

He's right. But the tremor still makes you nervous. Suddenly, going deeper into this waking volcano seems like a really bad idea.

"Let's return to your station," you say. "My team can look over the data you've collected."

You and Maria spend the next several days poring over the seismic data. Back in the United States, Isaac and your team run simulations. There is no doubt—the volcano is about to blow. You phone Dr. Brooks to report your findings.

"I'm looking at your data," Dr. Brooks says. "I'm not sure I see anything new here. It looks like we might have an eruption, but you can't tell us when or where."

"I feel like something big is coming," you argue. "Please, raise an alarm."

"I'm sorry," Dr. Brooks replies. "There's just not enough data to justify an evacuation. Your mission is over. Come home. We'll send the helicopter to get you."

You're on an airplane headed back to the United States when it happens. A volcano off the coast of China erupts. The underwater volcano creates a tsunami that kills thousands. You can only watch the devastation on television, knowing that your job was to prevent such a disaster—and you failed.

THE END

To read another adventure, turn to page 11.
To learn more about Volcanoes, turn to page 101.

You take a deep breath. "Okay," you say. "Let's see what's going on down there."

The ice cave winds deep into the mountain. As you go deeper, the chill of the surface disappears. Soon, you find that you're sweating, even with your parka unzipped.

"Is this heat normal?" you ask.

Vlad shakes his head. "No. I came down here a month ago. It was cold."

Suddenly, the ground begins to tremble. The minor earthquake lasts just a moment, but you hear the sound of rocks falling far in the distance.

"Do you think it's safe down here?" you ask.

Vlad shrugs. "A month ago, yes. Now? I do not know."

You've got some very sensitive instruments in your backpack. Some will measure movements below the surface. Others can sense changes in the levels of gasses like sulfur dioxide and carbon dioxide. These gasses can often signal an eruption. The closer you can get the equipment to the lava flow, the better readings you'll get. But do you dare risk going deeper into the cave with the entire mountain feeling so unstable?

To turn back, turn to page 33.

To go deeper into the mountain, turn to page 35.

"Stay calm," you tell yourself. You can't just leave. The research Vlad has collected is too valuable, and you need your phone to call for help. "Everyone, grab what you can!" you shout. "We have to get out of here. Go!"

It's a mad dash. You scoop up your phone and your laptop and stuff them into your backpack. Vlad grabs some of his research. Maria, Nadya, and Peter all cram what they can into their packs. Then you all throw your parkas on and run outside. The hissing and cracking of the cooling lava and the vaporizing ice is deafening.

"Hurry! Get on the snowmobiles," Vlad says, gesturing to four machines parked outside.

Nadya and Maria hop onto one snowmobile together. You, Peter, and Vlad each climb onto your own. The motors rev and soon you're racing across the rugged, snowy terrain.

Turn the page.

When a volcano erupts, its hot lava can quickly melt snow and ice on the mountain. This often creates dangerous flows of superheated mud and steam.

31

Wind blasts at your face as the lava flow gains on you from behind. It's a terrifying hour as the five of you zoom across the snowy landscape toward stable ground.

Finally, Vlad stops. "We should be safe now," he says. "The crust is thicker and more stable here."

You climb off the snowmobiles, huffing and panting. Thank goodness you brought your phone. Without it, no one would even know that you survived.

THE END

To read another adventure, turn to page 11.
To learn more about Volcanoes, turn to page 101.

You've seen enough. The temperature here tells you that the magma under the earth is getting close to the surface.

"Let's go, Vlad," you say.

The two of you scramble back to the cave entrance. Bitter cold hits you as you emerge from the cave and climb back onto your snowmobile.

You spend the next day analyzing the data Vlad and his team have collected. You run simulations based on what you know. The conclusion is inescapable. Earth's Pacific Plate is moving, creating instability all along the Pacific Rim. You call Dr. Brooks with your findings.

"My models show that we are seeing major flows of magma just below the surface," you tell her. "I think the entire region is unstable. My recommendation is to start evacuating people as soon as possible.

Turn the page.

Dr. Brooks takes your warning to the Russian government, but they are not convinced. "They didn't think there was enough data to support an evacuation," she explains.

You and Vlad's team spend the next week collecting more data. You need more proof. You send Dr. Brooks daily reports. A few small zones are evacuated. But when the day comes, it's not nearly enough. A shift in the Pacific Plate sets off eruptions from Siberia to Japan.

By the time it happens, it's too late to evacuate. Tens of thousands of people die as earthquakes and eruptions shake the land. The disaster is bigger than even you had imagined.

You did all you could to save lives. You just wish you could have done more.

THE END

To read another adventure, turn to page 11.
To learn more about Volcanoes, turn to page 101.

The earthquakes, the rising magma . . . something big is happening here. You need to know more.

"We may not have another opportunity like this," you say. "Let's keep going." The two of you travel deeper into the mountain. You take off your parka. Even in a T-shirt, you're sweating. "It must be 100 degrees down here," you say.

Vlad just nods. Another small tremor makes the ground shake.

"I think we cannot go any farther," Vlad says nervously.

He's right. You kneel down, placing sensors on the rock below. They'll measure changes in temperature and pressure below the surface, allowing you to create images of the lava flows below. Vlad speaks to Maria on a walkie-talkie.

Turn the page.

"We have a connection," Maria says. "You two should get out of there. The seismograph is starting to show a lot of activity."

"She's right," you say. "Let's get—"

Another tremor cuts you off. The rock below you shifts and cracks. Within seconds, the temperature rises another 20 degrees.

"We have to go!" Vlad shouts.

You don't argue. You turn and start to run. But as you sprint toward the cave entrance, you realize Vlad is no longer behind you.

"Help!" you hear from deeper in the cave. Vlad must have fallen.

Another tremor shakes the ground, and you hear a terrifying cracking noise. You want to help Vlad, but you also need to let the research team know what's happening.

In cold regions, the underground heat from a volcano can melt snow and ice to create caves. These ice caves are often unstable or can hold pockets of poisonous gases.

To turn back and find Vlad, turn to page 39.

To send a warning about the volcano, turn to page 41.

You nod at Vlad and he takes off. You sit down on the snowmobile, trying to remember how it works. It takes you a few moments to find the starting switch. The lava cracks and sizzles loudly, moving closer by the second. Finally, you start the motor. But as soon as you hit the throttle, the engine dies.

"NO!" you shout. Desperately, you try to restart the snowmobile. The engine sputters to life for a moment, but then dies again.

It's too late. The lava is here. There is no escape for you.

THE END

To read another adventure, turn to page 11.
To learn more about Volcanoes, turn to page 101.

"Vlad!" you shout.

The ground is shaking. The sound of falling rocks is deafening. But you can't leave Vlad behind. You charge back into the cave and find him lying on the ground, holding his leg. It's jammed into a deep crack that has opened in the floor of the cave.

"I think it's broken," Vlad cries.

Another tremor shakes the cave. The temperature is rising by the minute. Somewhere not far below your feet, the magma under this volcano is rising. Sweat pours down your face and soaks your clothes.

There's no time. You grab Vlad's trapped leg and pull. He screams in pain before passing out. You pull again, desperate to get out of here. Finally, his leg comes free. It's crushed and

Turn the page.

mangled. He couldn't put any weight on it even if he was conscious.

You grab Vlad under the arms and try to drag him out. But the extreme heat leaves you light headed. The ground shakes once again, and rocks above the cave's entrance tumble down in a loud crash.

You're trapped! Desperately, you try to contact the team back at the outpost to call for help and warn them. But all you hear is static. You don't know if they got the warning or not. Vlad is unconscious next to you. And soon you will be as well. You'll never get out of this cave alive. All you can do is hope your team will warn Dr. Brooks and people in the area of the disaster that lies ahead.

THE END

To read another adventure, turn to page 11.
To learn more about Volcanoes, turn to page 101.

You start back into the cave, but the heat is growing by the moment. You can't go any farther. You'll pass out if you stay any longer—and someone has to get a warning out to your team. "I'm sorry, Vlad!" you shout as you continue toward the cave entrance.

Behind you, the sound of the cave collapsing is deafening. You can feel the intense heat scorching your eyebrows. You're close to passing out. But you press on. Finally, when you feel like you can't run anymore, you see it. The cave opening. You burst out into the bitter cold, gasping for breath.

You wait for several minutes, hoping Vlad will emerge from the cave. But he doesn't.

You can't wait any longer. You hop onto one of the snowmobiles and speed back to the research station. You have to warn Dr. Brooks.

Turn the page.

"This volcano is about to erupt," you tell her over the phone. "And I don't think it will be the only one. The entire region could be at risk."

Your data is enough to convince her. "We'll get the warning out immediately," she promises. And it's just in time. When the eruptions do come, they are massive. But thanks to you, thousands of people have moved out of harm's way. Your warning saves countless lives. But you'll never forget the one you couldn't save. The sound of Vlad's calls for help will haunt you for the rest of your life.

THE END

To read another adventure, turn to page 11.
To learn more about Volcanoes, turn to page 101.

The lava flow is bearing down on you. There's no time! Maria, Nadya, and Peter have already taken two of the snowmobiles and are racing toward safety. You need to go too.

"Let's go, Vlad!" you shout.

You stop long enough to grab your parka. Then you're off on the last two snowmobiles left at the station. The vehicles zip over the snow and ice as you speed away from the eruption.

Earthquakes shake the ground below you. All you can do is ride, putting as much distance as possible between you and the volcano.

About an hour later, your snowmobile runs out of gas. You hop onto Vlad's machine, but it soon runs out of gas too. That's when you realize that you're stranded out here, in frozen Siberia.

Turn the page.

The Siberia region in northeastern Russia is famous for its long, brutally cold winters. Nighttime temperatures often fall below minus 80 degrees Fahrenheit (minus 62 degrees Celsius.)

You have no phone. No way to call for help. Even if someone came looking for you, they'd never find you.

Your fingers and toes are already feeling numb. Your nose is frostbitten. And as the sun dips toward the horizon, you know it's only going to get colder.

You won't survive the night.

THE END

To read another adventure, turn to page 11.
To learn more about Volcanoes, turn to page 101.

Peter, Maria, and Nadya have already left on snowmobiles. You have only seconds. You haven't ridden a snowmobile in years. Will you even remember how to start one? Just as Vlad begins to leave, you fling yourself onto the back of his snowmobile. You hold on for your life as he speeds away, twisting and turning along the ice-packed ground.

Vlad is a skilled driver. He expertly weaves his way over the rough land, putting distance between you and the lava flow. Your heart is racing so fast that you barely feel the bitter cold. But as you gain some distance, you realize that not bringing your parka was a serious mistake.

You use your phone to call the USGS for help.

"A helicopter is on the way," says the voice on the other end. But it could take some time for them to reach you. Already, you're shivering.

The next 45 minutes are brutal. The ground shakes with a series of earthquakes. The sky darkens with ash and smoke. You and Vlad take turns wearing his parka. Your skin starts to turn blue. Your teeth chatter while your body shivers violently.

Finally, you hear the whirring of an approaching helicopter. You're frostbitten. You have hypothermia. Your body is on the brink of collapsing. But help is here. As medics put you onto a stretcher and load you into the helicopter, you drift off to sleep. You're going to make it, but the ordeal has taken a serious toll on your body. It's an adventure you'll never forget.

THE END

To read another adventure, turn to page 11.
To learn more about Volcanoes, turn to page 101.

Hawaii is famous for its green mountains and lush, tropical forests. But it is also home to some of the world's biggest and most active volcanoes.

CHAPTER 3
HOT SPOT

Your airplane begins its descent into Hilo Airport in Hawaii. Through the window you notice the haze hanging over the state's biggest island. It's almost like a thin cloud covering the southeastern part of the island. After your plane touches down, you find a woman waiting for you.

"Hello," she says. "I'm Akela. I'm a ranger with the National Parks system here on the Big Island."

"Nice to meet you, Akela," you reply and then introduce yourself. "This is Maria," you continue, gesturing to the woman at your side.

Maria smiles. "The rest of our team is back on the mainland, ready to analyze whatever data we can collect."

Turn the page.

You leave the airport in Akela's jeep. Despite the haze that hangs over the island, it's a beautiful day.

"The air is not usually like this," Akela says. "But it's been a very active spring for the volcanoes. Kīlauea has always been active, but its eruptions have been growing over the past few weeks. And now Mauna Loa is starting to act up as well. It's making a lot of people here very nervous. It's rare for both volcanoes to be this active at the same time."

You're familiar with all of Hawaii's volcanoes. But you're eager to get Akela's point of view on them. "Tell me about them," you say.

"I spend most of my time around Kīlauea," Akela says. "It doesn't look the way most people expect volcanoes to look. It's flatter and lava flows from several vents along its rift zones.

"Mauna Loa is a more traditional volcano," Akela continues. "It's a monster. It's the world's largest volcano above sea level. It's also thought to be much older than Kīlauea. But even when it's active, Mauna Loa is usually pretty calm. It doesn't have the wild, unpredictable swings that Kīlauea has."

You'd love to study both volcanoes up close, as well as the others on this island. But time is critical. You need to figure out what's going on. Kīlauea's higher level of activity might make it the ideal volcano to study. On the other hand, Mauna Loa is the biggest volcano around. It might help you understand what's happening to the Pacific Rim.

To investigate Kīlauea, turn to page 52.
To head for Mauna Loa, turn to page 53.

"I'd like to see Kīlauea up close," you say.

Maria agrees. "We need to figure out why this island is so active. Kīlauea is our best bet."

Akela drives to the southeastern part of the island. "This isn't what I expected," Maria says. "When I think of Hawaii, I picture lush tropical forests. The land here is dry and barren."

Akela tells you more about the volcano. If you go one way, you can check out some of the volcano's lava tubes—tunnels that lava once flowed through. They can be dangerous though. You never know how strong the rock is beneath your feet. Or you could continue on to the summit caldera. It's the opening at the volcano's highest point. That's where a lot of the action is happening right now.

To explore the lava tubes, turn to page 56.
To investigate the summit caldera, turn to page 59.

The monster volcano that is Mauna Loa has always fascinated you. If this massive, ancient volcano is growing more active, that spells trouble. Perhaps some new measurements could help you figure out what's happening there.

Akela's house is along the way. She makes a quick stop to pick up her dog, Scout. The black lab is happy to greet you. He makes himself at home on your lap.

The drive up to Mauna Loa feels strange. The roads are abandoned. You don't see another vehicle. People living here seem to sense when something is happening. Most have cleared out to the more stable north side of the island.

You follow the road as far as you can. Then you continue on foot. Scout races out ahead as you work through the dense forest trail.

Turn the page.

"The hike to the summit is very difficult to do in one day," Akela warns you.

You smile. "I'm not interested in the summit today." You pull out a map of the region. "Here. This is where I'd like to go. To this rift zone."

The rift zones are places where the volcano is being pulled apart. They're often the most active parts of a volcano.

It's a long hike, but it's worth it. The dark black rock of past lava flows stands in sharp contrast to the soil that surrounds it. As you approach one of the biggest rifts, you gasp. Lava is flowing through the rift zone. It will be a great place to take readings. But getting that close to the lava could be dangerous.

To get closer to the flowing lava, turn to page 63.
To study from a safer location, turn to page 72.

Red-hot lava flows from an underground
rift zone near Mount Kīlauea.

"Let's go to the lava tubes," you reply.

You're carrying sensors that can take detailed readings of the ground under the volcano. They also detect changes in levels of certain gases that could signal an eruption. You want to get some readings from deep inside the volcano. Old lava tubes, like caves cut into the volcanic rock, could be the perfect way to get what you need.

Akela steers the jeep off-road along a flat, dusty plain. In the distance, smoke rises from one of the volcano's calderas.

"We're here," Akela says, pulling up to a stop.

At first, you're not sure why she's stopping. You don't see any place to enter a lava tube on this flat landscape. But then you see it, a small hole in the otherwise featureless plain.

"It's a skylight," she explains. "It's where the top of a lava tube has collapsed." She attaches a rope to the hitch of her jeep and tosses the other end down the opening. "It's only a dozen feet down. Follow me."

The two of you easily climb down into the lava tube. Maria, who has a fear of tight spaces, stays on the surface.

The tube is big enough inside to walk in. You pull out a flashlight and look in both directions. The tube is long, and mostly straight. You begin walking, searching for the perfect place to take some readings.

You wipe away some sweat from your forehead. It's hot down here.

"That's strange," Akela says. "I've been down here lots of times, and it's never been this hot."

Turn the page.

Suddenly, the ground below your feet shudders. A loud groaning sound echoes through the long lava tube.

"Was that an earthquake?" you ask, setting the backpack holding your equipment on the ground.

Akela shakes her head. "I'm not sure. This is unusual. Maybe we shouldn't be down here right now."

You're here for a reason. You need to figure out what's going on below the surface. But it might not be safe to stay here.

To place your sensors, turn to page 61.
To leave the lava tube, turn to page 65.

"Let's go to the summit caldera," you say. "I want to see what's happening at the center of the volcano."

Kīlauea's summit caldera has fascinated you for a long time. In 2018, part of the caldera floor collapsed. Water began to pool there, forming a lake in the crater.

"The water in the lake is gone now," Akela says. "It disappeared soon after this new activity began. The summit caldera is filled with lava again."

The three of you make your way toward the caldera. The location is closed off to tourists. It's a dangerous hike on unstable ground. But as a ranger, Akela makes her way confidently. You follow her lead.

The caldera is breathtaking.

"Look at that," Maria says with a gasp.

Turn the page.

A churning, bubbling lava lake stands in the heart of the caldera. Even from a distance, you can feel the heat pouring off of the volcano.

You stand just beyond the rim of the caldera. You could place your sensors here and move along. It's the safe choice. Or you could venture down into the caldera itself. It's risky but getting closer would mean getting better readings from your sensors. They could give you a better glimpse of what's going on below.

To place your sensors here, turn to page 67.
To venture deeper into the caldera, turn to page 70.

"I just need a few minutes to place the sensors," you say, kneeling down and unzipping your backpack. "Then we can get out of here."

The sensors detect small movements in the earth's crust, changes in temperature, and the levels of gasses. Every bit of data is important to help the team predict an eruption. You place the sensors firmly on the floor of the lava tube and activate them.

Suddenly, the ground shakes. You hear a thunderous cracking sound. Akela gasps.

"The tube is collapsing!" she screams. "Run!"

A crack is opening along the floor of the tube. Suddenly, the entire lava tube is glowing bright orange.

You try to run for the skylight. But it's too late. Red-hot lava surges up into the tube from below.

Turn the page.

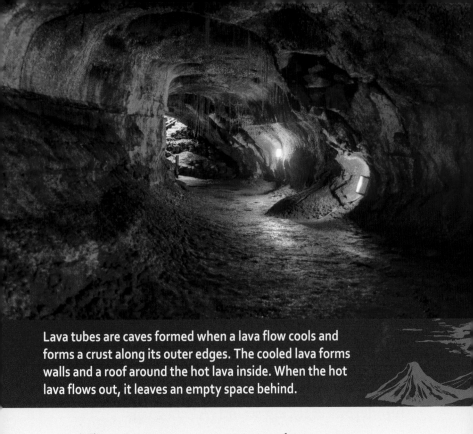

Lava tubes are caves formed when a lava flow cools and forms a crust along its outer edges. The cooled lava forms walls and a roof around the hot lava inside. When the hot lava flows out, it leaves an empty space behind.

The temperature soars, scorching your eyebrows. The rising lava blocks off your exit. And it slowly flows in your direction.

You take Akela's hand. There's nowhere to run. You just hope the end will be quick.

THE END

To read another adventure, turn to page 11.
To learn more about Volcanoes, turn to page 101.

"Let's get out of here," Akela says, tugging on your arm. Scout is ranging ahead, closer to the lava. Akela calls him back with fear in her voice.

"Just wait," Maria says. "Our models said that we might be seeing some flow in the rift zones. We might be on the right track."

Akela looks concerned, but she nods her head. "Let's be quick, then."

Maria and Akela watch nervously as you move closer. The lava glows orange through a black crust as it slowly winds down the valley. It's beautiful. You move alongside the river of lava, searching for the perfect spot to place your sensor.

Suddenly, Scout starts barking and darting around frantically.

Turn the page.

"I don't like this," Akela warns. "Scout only barks like this when he senses danger."

Scout's warning makes you pause. But you know that if you can get just a little closer, the data you collect might be that much better. Is it worth the risk?

To place your sensor here and get out, turn to page 74.
To move closer to the lava, turn to page 76.

This isn't safe. You decide to take Akela's advice.

"You're right. Let's get out of here!" you shout.

The two of you dash back to the skylight. You give Akela a boost as she scrambles up the rope. A loud cracking sound echoes through the lava tube as you grab the rope for yourself. A new blast of intense heat fills the tube, singing the hair on your arms. The floor of the tube itself is cracking open, and molten red lava is oozing in.

You leap, grab the rope, and haul yourself up. Maria screams at you to hurry as she helps pull you up over the lip of the skylight.

"Go!" she shouts.

The three of you sprint to the jeep and speed away. Behind you, the entire tube is collapsing. The ground sinks and heaves from the pressure

Turn the page.

of the rising lava. You stay just ahead of the collapse, rushing toward higher and more stable ground. Finally safe, Akela stops the jeep and you both stare back at a changed landscape.

"That was way too close," Maria says.

You nod. You know you're lucky to be alive. But you lost all your gear in that tube.

There is nothing you can do here now. It's time to head back home. You tried your best to help, but you failed.

THE END

To read another adventure, turn to page 11.
To learn more about Volcanoes, turn to page 101.

You need to be smart. Going farther into the caldera isn't worth the risk. You open your backpack and place one of the sensors inside the rim. Within a few minutes, it's activated and sending data back to the mainland.

"Okay, let's go," you say. Just as you do, the lava lake begins to churn and spit lava. Huge gobs of the molten rock shoot up into the air and land with a splat on the volcanic slope below you. The earth shakes.

You waste no time hiking back to Akela's jeep. She wasn't kidding when she warned you about how unstable Kīlauea is. You can almost feel the amazing forces working under your feet. She drives you back to Hilo, where Maria checks the data and helps to update the volcanic models of the area.

"Look at that!" you say.

Turn the page.

Your sensors show that magma is flowing at shocking rates, just below the surface. But as you zoom out, the model becomes less accurate. You can't get any data beyond the big island.

You dial Dr. Brooks and report your findings.

"The models show that Kīlauea is about to erupt," you report. "And it looks like Mauna Loa might as well. We might need to evacuate the southern half of the island."

Dr. Brooks asks if your newest models tell you anything about the rest of the volcanoes in the Pacific. "Sorry," you reply. "I just don't have enough data."

A few days later Kīlauea erupts violently. Within a few days, Mauna Loa does too. A spectacular eruption blows away a large chunk of the mountain.

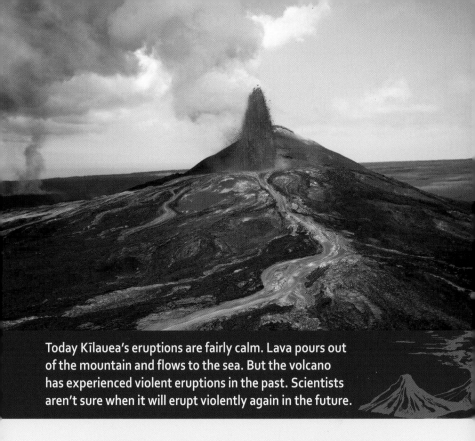

Today Kīlauea's eruptions are fairly calm. Lava pours out of the mountain and flows to the sea. But the volcano has experienced violent eruptions in the past. Scientists aren't sure when it will erupt violently again in the future.

Luckily, much of the southern half of the island was evacuated before the mountain blew. Your warning helped to save thousands of lives. You're proud that you helped to prevent the worst of the disaster.

THE END

To read another adventure, turn to page 11.
To learn more about Volcanoes, turn to page 101.

"We need to get the best readings we can. Everything depends on this," you say with a deep breath. "I need to get closer. Wait here."

Slowly, you make your way deeper into the caldera. The loose rocks slip beneath your feet. With every step, it gets hotter. But you know that every step you take means more accurate data for the sensor to gather.

You make it halfway into the caldera before you can't take it anymore. You're afraid you'll pass out from the intense heat if you go any farther. So you carefully place the sensor on the ground in a spot that seems somewhat stable.

When you stand back up, you feel dizzy. Suddenly, you're confused. Which way is up? You stumble and stagger in the wrong direction before realizing that you're going deeper toward the searing heat.

You're going to pass out. You'll never make it out of the caldera.

That's when you hear the footsteps. An arm slips around you. It's Akela. She helps you back up to the safety of the rim. She and Maria help carry you to safety, away from the heat of the volcano.

"Thanks," you tell them, catching your breath.

Back at the jeep, you check the data from the sensor so far. What you see is amazing. Magma is moving at alarming rates. The quality of your data helps the team build a model that shows that Hawaii is in danger of a series of eruptions.

"We've got to get the warning out right away," Maria says. "This data is going to save thousands of lives. Good work, everyone."

THE END

To read another adventure, turn to page 11.
To learn more about Volcanoes, turn to page 101.

You had expected to find lava flowing here. But now that you're standing so close, you feel a sense of panic. Is standing so close to a lava flow a smart idea? No, you tell yourself. This was a bad idea.

"Let's go," you agree. You'll get your sensor readings somewhere else. You don't want to put yourself or your colleagues at risk.

You spend the next few days at a volcano research station, studying the volcanoes. But without more data, it's difficult to run good models about what's happening. Dr. Brooks calls you. She's disappointed that you haven't come up with any answers. She says it's time for you to go home.

"But we're still watching the data come in," you explain. "I just need more time."

"We can monitor the data from here," Dr. Brooks replies. "I'm sorry you weren't able to collect the data you wanted. We'll do our best to predict any eruptions based on seismic data."

You try to argue, saying that you can do more. But Dr. Brooks has made up her mind. You've learned a lot about Hawaii's volcanoes, but you haven't really improved the USGS's ability to predict an eruption. You feel like you let everyone down and could have done more.

THE END

To read another adventure, turn to page 11.
To learn more about Volcanoes, turn to page 101.

Animals often sense danger before people do. Something has Scout spooked.

"Scout is saying it's time to get out of here," Akela says.

You decide to trust the dog's instincts. Quickly, you kneel down and place one of the sensors on the ground, near the lava flow. The high-tech gadget will give you a wealth of information about what's happening below the ground.

Maria checks her phone to make sure the sensor is transmitting. "Everything looks good. Now come on," she says.

The three of you and Scout head back away from the rift zone. Several more tremors shake the land. Each one is bigger than the last. You all pile into the jeep. Akela drives you away from the unstable volcano as quickly as she can.

Back at the research station, you look at the data. It shows massive movements of magma just a hundred feet below the surface. The pressure and temperature are rising fast. "I think Mauna Loa is about to erupt," you tell Akela.

It's time to call Dr. Brooks and tell her the news. Hawaii's volcanoes are about to erupt, and people need to evacuate right away.

Thousands of lives are at stake. People hurry to the north side of the island, away from the two volcanoes. You know the clock is ticking. It's possible that not everyone will make it to safety in time. But at least you've given them a chance.

THE END

To read another adventure, turn to page 11.
To learn more about Volcanoes, turn to page 101.

You scan the ground. It's not a perfect spot to place the sensor. You're looking for a flat, low-lying spot to collect the best data.

"Let's get closer," you say. You continue your trek along the lava flow. The ground shakes again. But this tremor is bigger and lasts much longer. Suddenly, the rock beneath your feet splits and begins to shift, knocking you to your knees. It's collapsing!

You try to scramble to your feet, but everything happens too quickly. The ground opens up beneath you. You grab the edge of the rock, barely clinging on with your fingertips. A sea of molten lava waits below to swallow you.

"Run!" you shout to Akela and Maria. "Get out of here!"

You can only hope they made it out. Because you know you won't. Your fingers are already

Geologists get close to lava flows in rift zones to study a volcano's behavior. It's risky work, but the data they gather helps them understand how volcanoes work and saves lives.

slipping off the ledge. You came to prevent a disaster. But now, your journey ends in one.

THE END

To read another adventure, turn to page 11.
To learn more about Volcanoes, turn to page 101.

CHAPTER 4

INTO THE DEPTHS

Still, blue water stretches out to the horizon in every direction. You and Maria, a member of your team, step off the helicopter that brought you 300 miles off the coast of Oregon. You're both amazed by the calm and beauty of the open ocean. You wish the rest of your team back on the mainland could see it.

"Hard to believe that under our feet is one of the most active underwater volcanoes in the Pacific Ocean, isn't it?" says Amir. The captain of the research vessel is a tall, slender man with a thick beard. You stand on the deck of his ship, which is loaded with high-tech research equipment.

Turn the page.

"We've been studying the Axial Seamount for months," says Dr. Michelle Andrews, the leader of the research team. "Our automatic submersible vehicles have given us detailed maps of its structure. But starting a few weeks ago, we noticed the volcano's activity increasing. And in the past week, it's erupting at an alarming level. It's not clear why."

"We need to see what's happening down there," you explain. "If a large eruption happens, it could cause a huge tsunami. It could destroy coastlines and kill thousands of people around the Pacific. Our models depend on detailed data, we just don't have a lot of that for these deep-sea volcanoes."

Dr. Andrews nods. "The good news is that we have everything you need here to investigate. The submarine can take you down to see the volcano up close. But the conditions are unpredictable."

Turn the page.

"Be safe—use one of the robots," says Kevin, a member of the research team in charge of the autonomous vehicles. "You can see anything you want underwater through the cameras. There's no need to risk going down there yourself."

You scratch your head, weighing your options.

"Can we get everything we need with the robot cam?" Maria asks. She has a fear of tight spaces, and you know there's no way she'd join you on the trip. To you, the idea of traveling to a volcano a mile beneath the ocean's surface is both thrilling and terrifying. Is it really worth the risk?

To use the robotic vehicle, turn to page 82.

To visit the volcano in the submarine, turn to page 84.

"This is the ROV," Kevin says as the crew prepares the high-tech robot. "It's short for Remotely Operated Vehicle."

You and Maria watch as a huge crane carefully lowers the ROV into the water. Kevin leads you to the bridge of the ship, where the ROV's control center is set up.

"We can steer it with this panel," Kevin says. He shows you how he controls the ROV, which is rapidly descending into the darkness of the deep ocean.

After a few minutes, the ROV approaches the ocean floor. The geothermal vents along the volcano's base are teeming with marine life. You see tube worms, sea spiders, and schools of fish. It's beautiful. But you really only have eyes for one thing: the volcano. It glows orange-hot as lava flows out of the volcano and into the sea.

You and Kevin spend an hour observing the volcano and measuring changes in temperature. You're getting a good look at the volcano, but it's not enough. You really wish that you'd gone down yourself.

"Take it up," you tell Kevin. You sit in silence as he brings the ROV back to the surface.

You could still take the submarine down and investigate up close. Or you could plug the new data into the models and see what you get. That would save you from having to make a scary, dangerous trip to the ocean floor.

"What do you think?" Dr. Andrews asks as she enters the bridge. "Did you get what you need?"

To take the submarine to get a better look, turn to page 84.

To decide you have enough data, turn to page 95.

You need to see what's happening with your own eyes. "Let's go down," you tell Dr. Andrews.

She nods. "I thought you might say that. We'll do all we can to keep you safe."

The crew and research team snap to work. Maria and Kevin work together to make sure the submarine's sensors are ready.

"The cabin is pressurized," Kevin explains. "If it wasn't, the weight of the water at those depths would crush the sub like a soda can."

Kevin notices your uneasy smile. "Don't worry. We'll be in constant contact and monitoring you on the sub's camera."

The submarine is meant for two people. Dr. Andrews joins you to operate the vehicle. You sit together in the cramped cabin as a crane lowers you into the water. With a jolt, the crane releases the sub and you begin to sink. It's an eerie feeling. Within moments, the water begins to filter out the sunlight, and darkness creeps in.

You slowly drop hundreds of feet below the surface. It's another world down here. The submarine's lights attract deep-sea fish.

As you go deeper, you see a faint orange glow.

"There's the caldera," Michelle says.

It's a stunning sight. Lava oozes out of the caldera. To either side you see the rifts, where the earth's crust is pulling apart.

"Can we get a closer look at the rifts?" you ask.

"We can, but it's risky," Michelle replies. "The rift zones are deep. Deeper than we've ever gone."

To move closer to the caldera, turn to page 87.
To investigate the depths of the rifts, turn to page 89.

Turn the page.

Small, two- to three-person submarines are designed to withstand the high pressure thousands of feet below the ocean's surface.

The caldera is the heart of the volcano. It churns and boils as super-heated lava collides with cool ocean water.

"How close can we get?" you ask.

Dr. Andrews smiles. "Just watch."

She guides the small submarine down toward the glowing caldera. The closer you get, the rougher the ride gets. "Currents of heated water make it a bit bumpy," Dr. Andrews explains.

The submarine is geared with cutting-edge technology. You're able to view the volcano in a range of different modes, including infrared. This light, generated from heat, isn't visible to the human eye. But the volcano glows brightly in the infrared. It shows you just how hot the volcano is.

"Show me the ground-penetrating radar," you say.

Turn the page.

Dr. Andrews hits a button and a new display pops up on the view screen. It shows you a detailed picture of what's happening beneath the volcano. A large magma chamber is swelling just below the volcano's surface.

You spend the next 10 minutes taking detailed measurements of the volcano. But they are changing almost minute-to-minute.

"I've never seen it like this," Dr. Andrews says. "I think we're looking at the start of a new eruption."

Watching an eruption would be the thrill of a lifetime, and you might learn a lot. But if it's violent, it could put the sub at risk.

To keep studying the volcano up close, turn to page 91.
To get back to the surface quickly, turn to page 92.

"Take me to the rift," you say.

Dr. Andrews hesitates. "Are you sure? We've never taken the sub that low before. It's within our limits, but why push it?

You nod. "We need to see what's happening. Lives could depend on it."

Dr. Andrews takes a deep breath and pilots the submarine deeper and deeper, down into the rift. There's a vibrant ecosystem down here. Giant sea spiders and tube worms cluster around the geothermal vents.

"It's beautiful," you whisper.

The rift looks like a deep valley cut into the sea floor. You use the submarine's thermal imaging to see hot spots along the rift. These are areas where the crust is very thin. One spot glows bright orange on the screen.

Turn the page.

"There," you say, pointing. "Let's get closer."

Down you go. The submarine creaks and groans with every foot you drop now. You both sit in silence, aware of the massive pressure pushing in on you from every side.

The submarine groans again. But this time it's followed by a crack. An alarm sounds.

"Something is wrong!" Kevin shouts through the radio. "Get up! Get up now! The sub can't take that much pressure! It's going to—"

It's too late. A stream of water sprays from the hatch. Then . . . the ocean crushes the submarine. Twisted metal and the unspeakable weight of the ocean crash in on you. Your last thought is about how you've failed your mission.

THE END

To read another adventure, turn to page 11.
To learn more about Volcanoes, turn to page 101.

You can't believe your luck. The Axial Seamount volcano will erupt soon. You're going to get real-time measurements. You couldn't have asked for more.

The caldera boils and churns. It spits out huge plumes of hot magma. The water gets rough, but the submarine is built to take a rough ride. You know that staying here could be dangerous. But you are both scientists who have devoted your lives to studying eruptions. You agree that it's worth the risk. You keep your instruments pointed at the eruption, letting them record the data.

In time, the volcano quiets. "We should go up," Dr. Andrews says.

You hate to leave. Now that the caldera has quieted, you'd love to move in for a closer look.

To head for the surface, turn to page 96.
To get a closer look, turn to page 98.

You start to feel a sense of panic.

"I don't like this," you tell Dr. Andrews. "I think we should get out of here."

"Kevin, we're headed up," she radios.

The submarine rises slowly. You continue to stare at the volcano as it belches out a huge burst of lava. The water gets choppy, and the submarine bucks and dips. For a moment, you're afraid Dr. Andrews will lose control of it. You can almost feel the pressure of the water this deep about to crush you.

But Dr. Andrews keeps a steady hand. Up, up, up you go. Soon, sunlight begins to trickle through the water. Then, with a burst, you surface, just a few hundred feet from the ship. The crew helps you back aboard.

Turn the page.

The West Mata volcano near Samoa and Fiji in the Pacific Ocean erupted violently in 2009. It is the deepest underwater volcanic eruption ever seen.

"Good work down there," Amir says. "But I'm surprised you left just when the volcano started to erupt. Isn't that exactly what you came to observe?"

You sigh. You know that the team here is collecting a lot of great data on the eruption below. You would have loved the chance to witness it firsthand. But staying alive is more important. Maybe someday you'll get another chance.

THE END

To read another adventure, turn to page 11.
To learn more about Volcanoes, turn to page 101.

Getting close to the volcano is too dangerous. The data you've collected will have to be enough.

You spend the next two days studying the data from the volcano. You run a series of models, but none explain why the volcano is behaving this way. It's impossible to predict when it will erupt.

When your phone rings and you see it's Dr. Brooks. "What has your team found?" she asks. "People here are getting nervous."

"Sorry," you reply. "I ran a dozen models, and they all turned out differently. I don't know where the eruptions are going to take place, or when."

Your adventure has ended in failure. If a disaster is coming, you haven't done anything to help save anyone from it.

THE END

To read another adventure, turn to page 11.
To learn more about Volcanoes, turn to page 101.

It's time to return to the surface. You've got more data than you could have ever hoped for.

"Let's go," you agree.

You're both all smiles as you make the slow climb to the surface. The crew greets you with cheers as you come back aboard the ship.

"Well done," Amir says.

You get straight to work, plugging the new data into the computerized models. Everything begins to take shape. Your worst fears are confirmed. Magma is moving in ways you've never seen before. The Pacific Plate is on the move.

"I think we could be looking at a series of eruptions," you tell Dr. Brooks. "If that happens, there's a high risk of tsunamis all along the Pacific. It's almost impossible to know where they could strike."

"Thank you," Dr. Brooks says. "I will speak to the White House immediately."

Over the next few days, you remain aboard the ship, continuing to study the volcano. Meanwhile, people all along the coastlines of the Pacific prepare. When the eruptions come, most of them are ready. Several tsunamis strike the Pacific. They cause a great deal of damage to coastlines, but the human death toll is low—all thanks to your warning.

THE END

To read another adventure, turn to page 11.
To learn more about Volcanoes, turn to page 101.

This is a once-in-a-lifetime opportunity, you think to yourself.

You've been fascinated with volcanoes since you were a kid. And now you have the chance to get up close to one.

"Take us in closer," you say quietly.

Dr. Andrews hesitates. "Are you sure? You've got all the data you need now, don't you?"

"Just a little bit," you say. "Look at it. It's beautiful."

Dr. Andrews bites her lip and pilots the sub in closer to the orange-hot caldera. The water churns here as the molten rock heats it.

Suddenly, an alarm sounds.

"Pressure alert!" Dr. Andrews shouts. Quickly, she tries to bring the submarine up.

But the sub is caught in a whirling current. You're flung sideways in the jet of fast-moving water. The sub dips lower and lower, closer to the caldera.

Dr. Andrews flips a switch and pulls hard on the control. Suddenly the submarine spins and breaks free of the current.

"That was too close," you say, letting out a gasp of air. If not for Dr. Andrews's quick thinking and skill, you would have both perished in the heart of the volcano. You didn't get as close to the volcano as you wanted. But the data you collected will help you understand what's happening here.

THE END

To read another adventure, turn to page 11.
To learn more about Volcanoes, turn to page 101.

TECTONIC PLATES

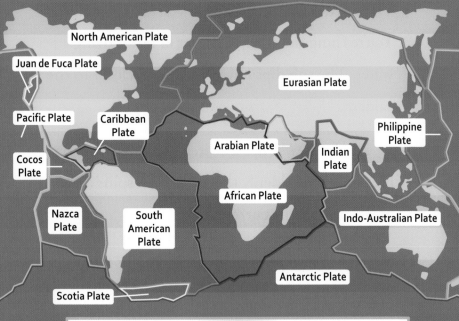

North American Plate

Juan de Fuca Plate

Eurasian Plate

Pacific Plate

Caribbean Plate

Philippine Plate

Arabian Plate

Indian Plate

Cocos Plate

African Plate

Nazca Plate

South American Plate

Indo-Australian Plate

Antarctic Plate

Scotia Plate

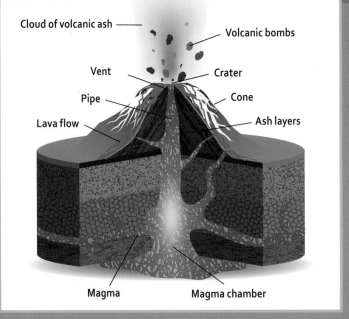

Cloud of volcanic ash

Volcanic bombs

Vent

Crater

Pipe

Cone

Lava flow

Ash layers

Magma

Magma chamber

CHAPTER 5

VOLCANOES AND TECTONIC PLATES

It's easy to think of the Earth's surface as being solid and stable. But the truth is that the outer layer of the planet, called the crust, is quite complex. Earth's crust is divided into seven major sections, or plates. These plates sit on top of a layer of liquid magma called the mantle. The plates shift, move, and collide with one another.

As the plates move, so does the magma below. In places, magma rises up through the crust. When it flows from a volcano onto the earth's surface, it's called lava.

Most of the world's volcanoes lie along the edges of the largest plate, the Pacific Plate. Scientists believe this plate is drifting northwest at about 2.75 inches (7 centimeters) per year. That doesn't sound like much. But it creates a lot of pressure along the plate's boundaries. That helps to create a long chain of volcanoes called the Ring of Fire that follow the edges of the massive Pacific Plate. Other volcanoes, including those that created the islands of Hawaii, are formed by hot spots on the plate, where magma rises to the surface.

Scientists are continually working to learn more about the movements of the plates and how they trigger volcanic eruptions. They use scientific instruments such as seismographs to measure the movements of the crust. Some scientists build computer models to predict where and when volcanic eruptions might happen. The USGS is one organization that studies this data. They work to learn as much about volcanoes as they can.

In this story, the Pacific Plate started moving more rapidly than normal. Could it really happen? It's difficult to say. Scientists are constantly learning new and surprising things about tectonic plates. What if the Pacific Plate did start to move quickly? It could trigger a huge disaster. Undersea volcanoes and earthquakes could create huge tsunamis, like the one that struck Japan in 2011. That disaster caused more than 22,000 casualties. Volcanoes above the surface could spew huge amounts of ash into the air.

Earth's history is filled with massive volcanic events. Could another one happen along the Ring of Fire? Could a super-volcano such as Yellowstone erupt violently and change life on Earth? Scientists are working hard to predict such a disaster long before it happens. They hope to give people plenty of warning to avoid the devastation.

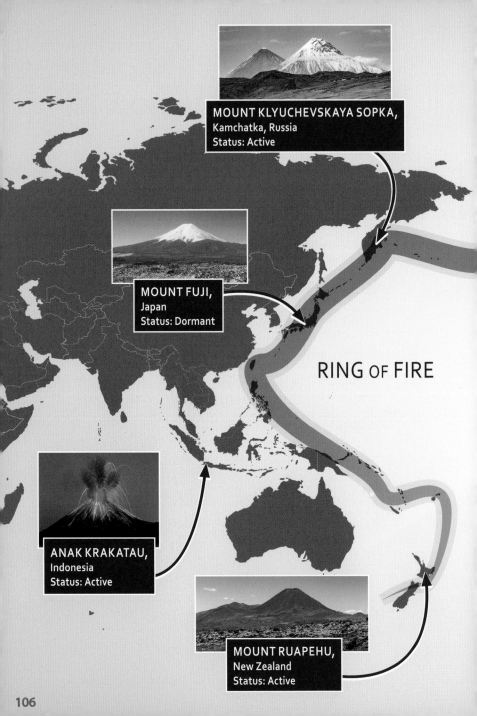

MOUNT KLYUCHEVSKAYA SOPKA,
Kamchatka, Russia
Status: Active

MOUNT FUJI,
Japan
Status: Dormant

RING OF FIRE

ANAK KRAKATAU,
Indonesia
Status: Active

MOUNT RUAPEHU,
New Zealand
Status: Active

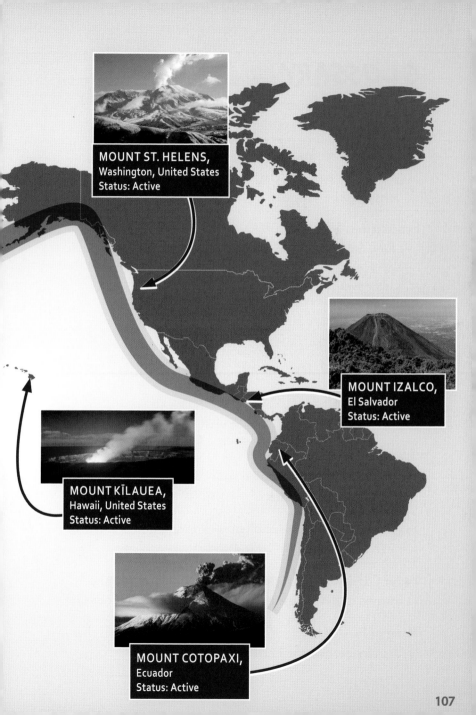

MOUNT ST. HELENS,
Washington, United States
Status: Active

MOUNT IZALCO,
El Salvador
Status: Active

MOUNT KĪLAUEA,
Hawaii, United States
Status: Active

MOUNT COTOPAXI,
Ecuador
Status: Active

GLOSSARY

caldera (kal-DAYR-uh)—a large depression resulting from the collapse of the center of a volcano

dormant (DOR-muhnt)—quiet, but still active; dormant volcanoes have not erupted for many years, but could erupt in the future

evacuation (i-VA-kyuh-WAY-shuhn)—the removal of large numbers of people from an area during a time of danger

extinct (ek-STINGKT)—no longer active; extinct volcanoes have not erupted for thousands of years and are unlikely to erupt again

geothermal (jee-oh-THUR-muhl)—relating to the intense heat inside the earth

infrared (in-fruh-RED)—light waves that are invisible to human eyes

lava (LAH-vuh)—hot, liquid rock that comes from a volcano when it erupts

magma (MAG-muh)—molten rock found under the earth's surface

radar (RAY-dar)—an electronic device that uses radio waves to determine the location or shape of an object

Ring of Fire (RING OF FIRE)—a line of volcanoes that circles around the Pacific Ocean

seismograph (SIZE-muh-graf)—a device used to measure the strength and direction of earthquakes and other vibrations in the earth's crust

seismology (size-MOL-uh-jee)—the study of earthquakes

simulation (sim-yuh-LAY-shuhn)—a computer model of something in real life

tectonic plates (tek-TON-ik PLAYTS)—giant slabs of earth's crust that move around on magma; the earth has nine major tectonic plates, as well as many minor plates.

tsunami (tsoo-NAH-mee)—a large, destructive wave caused by an underwater earthquake or eruption

OTHER PATHS TO EXPLORE

>>> In the story, a volcanic disaster is about to occur. How would you feel about the news if you were living near a volcano or along the Ring of Fire? Where would you go? What would you take with you?

>>> Many scientists spend their lives studying volcanoes. Big eruptions give them a chance to learn more about how and why volcanoes behave the way they do. If you devoted your career to studying these natural events, would you be excited about all you could learn from a big eruption? Or would you be more worried about the devastation it could cause?

>>> Imagine if the main character in the story was wrong about big eruptions coming. How would you feel if you started one of the biggest evacuations in human history . . . and then nothing happened? Would you be embarrassed? Relieved? Disappointed?

READ MORE

Doyle, Abby Badach. *Plate Tectonics Reshape Earth!* New York: Gareth Stevens Publishing, 2021.

Gibbons, Gail. *Volcanos!* New York: Holiday House, 2021.

Hoena, B. A. *Can You Survive a Supervolcano Eruptuon?: An Interactive Doomsday Adventure.* North Mankato, MN: Capstone Press, 2016.

Klepeis, Alicia. *The Science of Volcanic Eruptions.* New York: Cavendish Square, 2020.

INTERNET SITES

NASA Space Place: Tectonic Forces
spaceplace.nasa.gov/tectonics-snap/en/

National Geographic Kids: Volcanoes
kids.nationalgeographic.com/explore/science/volcano/

ScienceKids: Earth Science
www.sciencekids.co.nz/earth.html

Smithsonian Museum of Natural History
naturalhistory.si.edu/

INDEX